Words to Know Before You Read

sail

sailboat

sandals

sea

seals

seashore

see

sizes

sound

suits

surf

surfboards

surrounded

www.rourkeeducationalmedia.com

Edited by Luana Mitten
Illustrated by Marc Mones
Art Direction, Cover and Page Layout by Tara Raymo

Library of Congress PCN Data

Surfing Safari / Precious McKenzie
ISBN 978-1-62169-253-9 (hard cover) (alk. paper)
ISBN 978-1-62169-211-9 (soft cover)
Library of Congress Control Number: 2012952749

Rourke Educational Media
Printed in the United States of America,
North Mankato, Minnesota

rourkeeducationalmedia.com

customerservice@rourkeeducationalmedia.com • PO Box 643328 Vero Beach, Florida 32964

Surfing Safari

Counselor
Lou

Will

Viv

Rosie

Nia

Written By Precious McKenzie
Illustrated By Marc Mones

"We are off to the seashore, campers!" shouts Counselor Lou.

"HOORAY!" the children cheer.

"Will we sail on a sailboat?" asks Viv.

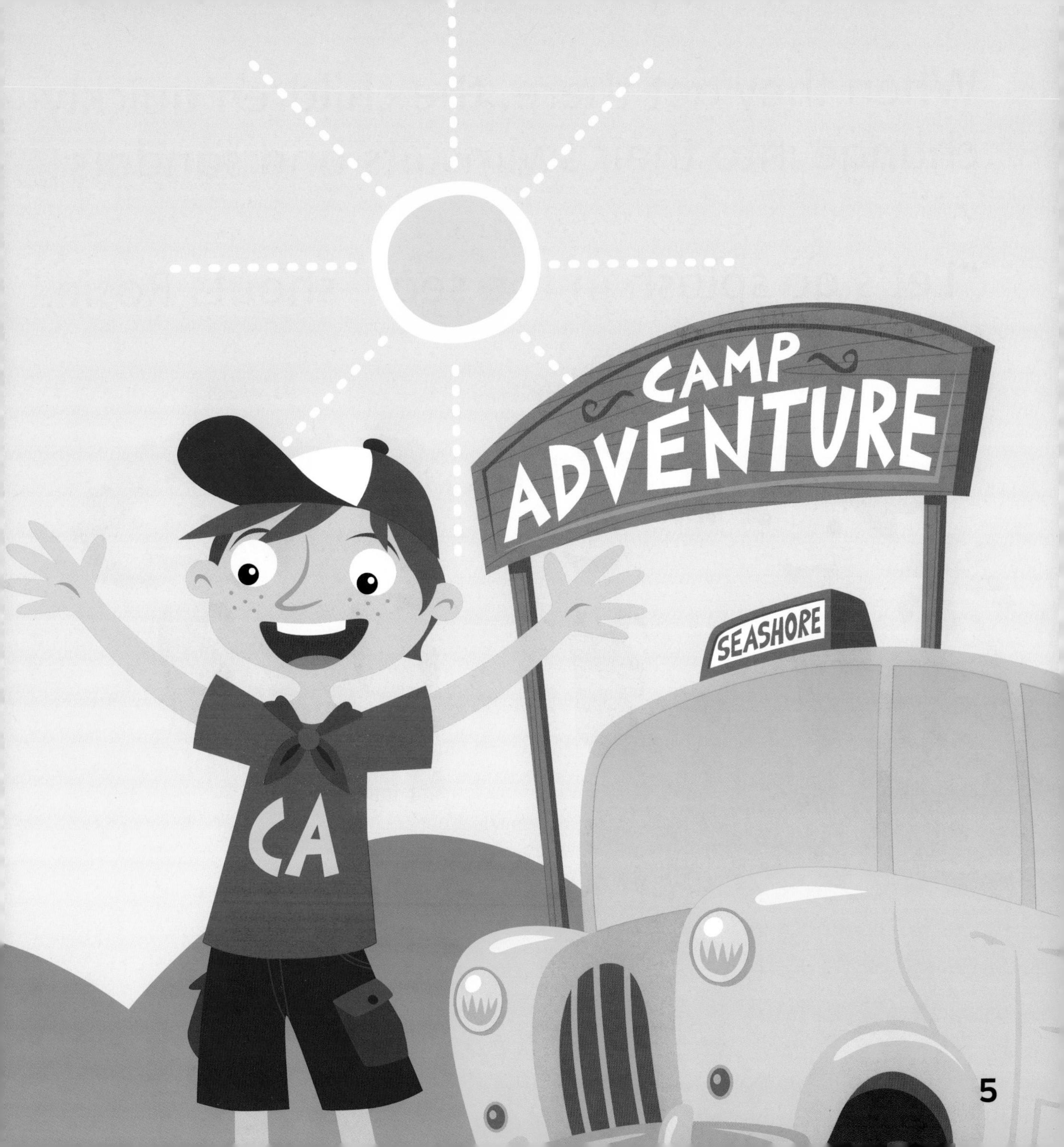
CAMP ADVENTURE
SEASHORE
CA

When they get there, the children quickly change into their swimsuits and sandals.

"Let's go splash in the sea!" shouts Rosie.

"Look, surfboards of all shapes and sizes!" calls Will.

"Let's surf in the sea," says Nia.

"Put on your wetsuits first," calls Counselor Lou. "The deep sea could be cold."

Nia and Will splash in the sea with their sleek surfboards.

They sit and wait for a big wave.

Soon they are surrounded by fins.

"SHARKS!" shouts Will.

"Surf for the shore!" yells Nia.

15

Nia slides off her surfboard. SPLASH!

"Quick, grab my hand!" shouts Will.

Nia hops on Will's surfboard. They see the shore.

"Can we swim faster than sharks?" Will asks.

Then they hear a silly sound.

BARK! BARK!
BARK! BARK!

"Seals!" they shout.

After Reading Word Study

Picture Glossary

Directions: Look at each picture and read the definition. Write a list of all of the words you know that start with the same sound as *sea*. Remember to look in the book for more words.

sailboat (SAYL-boht): A sailboat is a boat that moves through the water with the help of wind blowing through its large sail.

sandals (SAN-duhlz): Sandals are open shoes that have straps which go over the feet.

sea (SEE): The sea is a large body of water.

seals (SEELZ): Seals are mammals that live near coasts. They have thick fur and flippers.

seashore (SEE-shor): The seashore is the sandy or rocky land that touches the sea.

surfboards (SURF –bordz): Surfboards are long boards that surfers stand on to ride the waves.

About the Author

Precious McKenzie lives in Billings, Montana, where she never sees seals at the seashore. But, she does see muskrats in shining streams.

Ask The Author!
www.rem4students.com

About the Illustrator

Marc Mones is a Spanish illustrator. He lives in Bolvir, a small town in the Pyrenees, with his wife Rose, his two sons Gerard and Martin, and his four cats. Marc has liked to draw since he was a little kid. His father is also an illustrator and his mother is a very good painter. His very favorite things to draw are monsters!

Comprehension & Word Study:

- Retell the Story: Sequence It

  What activity were the campers going to do in the story?

  What was the problem?

  What happened at the end?

  Did it surprise you?

  What else could it have been?

- Word Study: Surfing for Ss

  Have the children listen for words from the story with the Ss sound. Identify which words use the sound at the end of the word. Write the singular form of a word and the plural form of the word using –s at the end. How are the words the same? How are they different? Discuss how adding –s at the end of a word can change the meaning to show more than one.

Sound Adventures

Sound Words I Used:

sail
sailboat
sandals
sea
seals
seashore
see
sizes
suits
surf
surfboards
surrounded

Let's Learn The **Ss** Sound

Surfing Safari

Sound Adventures

Sound Adventures is a fresh approach to traditional phonics based readers. With delightful stories, they build vocabulary and encourage readers to apply what they are learning about letters and sounds. Come along on wild journeys with the characters from Camp Adventure!

ISBN 978-1-6216-9211-9

90000

9 781621 692119

Sound Adventures

by

Rourke
Educational Media
rourkeeducationalmedia.com

A Ship and Shells

Teaching Focus:

Word Hunt

Have children look for words that use the blend sh in books or other printed material around the room. List the words and add any others that the children might have to offer. Have volunteers help you circle or underline the letters that make that sound. If any children bring you words that only use s, then make a second list and have the children help you distinguish where each word should go. You could also give each child a sticky note and write down the words they find in the word hunt.

Teacher Notes available at
rem4teachers.com

Tips for Reading this Book with Children:

1. Read the title and make predictions about the story.

   Predictions – after reading the title have students make predictions about the book.

2. Take a picture walk.

   Talk about the pictures in the book. Implant the vocabulary as you take the picture walk.

   Have children find one or two words they know as they do a picture walk.

3. Have students look at the first pages of the book and find a word that begins with the letter or sound focus of the book.

4. Ask students to think of other words that begin with that same sound.

5. Strategy Talk – use to assist students while reading.
   - Get your mouth ready
   - Look at the picture
   - Think…does it make sense
   - Think…does it look right
   - Think…does it sound right
   - Chunk it – by looking for a part you know

6. Read it again.

7. Complete the activities at the end of the book.